# EAR CANDY

# EAR
# CANDY

## THE FETISH
## EDITION

A. AKIL

Allow me

to be

the first

to welcome you

to more naughty tales and

confessions

so flip over

it's side 2

This book is for the side of you

that you really can't explain.

That open side of you that needs

to be addressed by a totally different name like,

Hot CoCo, Cowboy, Sizzle or Raine

Now introduce your fetish name aloud as

Ear Candy's Fetish Edition once again

entertains.

# Contents

# I. *Confession*

You know that moment

The feeling-

The depth of overstanding that significant energy has arrived

without permission

and wants to

enter your universe

with a purpose and an exclamation point!

In the end, you find yourself needing a new name

after a complete identity change

because

life as you know it

can never be the same

Not after that.

Not after her.

— Wide Open

# Maple isn't just for Pancakes

They call me Maple. People have their own version of how I received my nickname. Some joke that I received the name because I am known to keep a heavy stash of maple syrup at my house. Others assume that it is either a childhood name that I received lovingly because of my complexion or from my love for pancakes.

The truth is, I haven't always kept a case of maple syrup stashed in my pantry, and I wasn't lovingly given the name from childhood. I am not called Maple because of my smooth amber-colored skin nor because of my rich and sweet personality. My nickname was birthed from some freaky events that took place on a Friday six years ago to this day.

I don't think that I will ever forget how I was initiated into "Maple", ten months after I relocated to Atlanta. I was reintroduced to Maple syrup more thoroughly than I had ever imagined. "Maple" changed life as I knew it, and there was no way that I could leave her behind. You see, the nickname was supposed to be an inside joke between Rodrigo and I, except he wasn't around long enough to get it.

# The Backstory of Maple

Rodrigo called out of the blue on a chilly Friday morning in October. I saw it as *out of the blue* because we had not spoken for about 9 months at the time. There was no bad blood between us, we just kind of fizzled out. Fizzled out as in, I eventually realized after months of the best sex I had experienced in my life, I had absolutely nothing in common with the person attached to the tool I had become so fond of.

Thankfully one day the sex haze lifted just long enough for me to notice that we had never had a full conversation. At the time, I wanted more substance. Turned out that it wasn't as insignificant as I thought and I ended up sometimes missing that piece in my life.

So, when I received his call it was an unexpected but pleasant surprise.

I immediately began reminiscing on how much I enjoyed our wild escapades. Afterall, he was unforgettable. It took me two and a half months just to take in all 13 of his inches…and I mean really take it all in. Once I could…wow. Our sexual chemistry was so on fire that it took me almost a year to realize that we had never been on a date! Yes, it was that dangerous dick. The dick that you need to control so that you won't be somewhere, outside someone's house, ready to pop the trunk and challenge the competition! I was finally able to get my head together and take a break from our love affair and I thought the feelings faded away.

That's why when I answered the unknown number it was an unexpected but pleasant surprise. I almost didn't answer but as chance would have it I did. "Hello?"

"Buen dia! You answered! Hola, Mami! It's been a long time. I miss you." A smooth velvety voice sounded off from the other side of the line.

"Si," I replied so fast that I couldn't help but wonder again whose voice spoke for me. I didn't even get a chance to think of my response! This is exactly why I stopped talking to him in the first place. I remembered how he makes me lose my self-control before I added:

"I miss you more."

"Will you come to my house

so that we can catch up?"

This is the time where I should have told him all about himself. I wanted to say no and explain that I deserved more than he had to offer. I also wanted to get off my chest that these antics were the reason I stopped talking to him in the first place because we never did any—

"I want to cook dinner for you," he stopped me in my tracks and shut down all of my doubtful thoughts.

I was already weak for him so adding what sounded to be a considerate gesture just wasn't fair.

"When do you want to do this?" I asked, with a slight attitude but secretly hoping that it was very soon.

"Tomorrow or even tonight if you aren't busy. Do you have plans?"

I looked over at my completely full wall calendar but before rationale kicked in, the unrecognizable voice that had taken control over my mouth earlier in the conversation struck again, "Well, it just so happens I am free tonight," a lie that I turned into the truth.

"Perfecto!" His voice was so excited. "Is 8pm okay? You tell me, it's whatever you want."

Yeah, he was laying the charm on thick, and I was eating it up. "Well, that's kind of late for me because I have an early morning…" Before I could finish he cut me off,

"Si Si Mami! I understand, it's just that I am planning something muy muy especial and I need enough time to prepare. Give me 7:45 por favor?" he pleaded.

"Mmm, I guess that will work," I agreed stubbornly as I slightly smiled and caressed my earlobe.

"Ok sweetie, great. I am really looking forward to seeing you tonight. It's been a long time, and I am going to make up for that." His voice sounded so damn sexy. The spanglish mixed with the aggressive commands was a mix that I called the "The Panty Dropper". All I could do was hope that "fucking the shit out of me" was on the menu tonight but kept it cool with a simple, "Ok, I can't wait to see you in the kitchen".

Oh my gosh, I know, that sounded so stupid. But the truth was I couldn't wait to see him in the kitchen. As I went up to my room to get dressed I wondered what he would be wearing. I envisioned him butt naked with an apron on. Then I saw him wearing only a chef's hat and Timberland boots. He switched to cowboy. I then pictured him with a cowboy hat pumping me on the counter with a spatula in his hand slapping my ass. Ok, ok! Do you see what I mean? He had that effect on me.

I rushed and canceled all of the things that I really had planned for that evening before his call.

When I finally got my head together and picked out my clothes, I dressed with intention. I wore the sexiest outfit that I owned. I forgot to ask if I should bring anything, so I decided to serve up some nice cleavage to compliment the dessert I planned to serve him after dinner. I decided to go with a short black dress that was known to bring a man to his knees. The fit was skintight to accentuate everything that I had to offer. I slid on my knee-length black leather red bottom boots on top of my silky black thigh highs. Before walking out the door I looked in the mirror with approval and grabbed a long sweater to protect all of my exposed assets from the fall breeze.

When I arrived at Rodrigo's building I was surprised to see the entry code was the same. As I entered 9110024 the meaning behind it made me giggle to myself. Once I approached his door I knocked softly but the music was so loud I had to give a few police bangs before I heard his loud footsteps head towards the door. He opened happily with a big smile, no shirt and linen pants.

Linen pants are my weakness. They hung just right on his body and the dick print was the star of the show. I immediately fell into his arms and gave him a hug. My hand briefly rubbed against the bulging print in his pants. He held me tight into his big and strong embrace. When he let go and our eyes locked -our lips did as well.

We kissed as if we were out of a love scene from a romance novel. So deep, so passionate, I immediately went for his zipper. To my surprise and disappointment, he stopped me. "Whoa! Whoa! Come in. Let me take your jacket." I giggled, realizing that I hadn't even stepped inside the door yet.

When I stepped into his entrance and took a look around, I was shocked and caught off guard. He had his entire loft covered in plastic. I was thinking, what the fuck did I just walk into?

6

He took the words out of my mouth when he said, "Oh this? Well, in the kitchen is the dinner that I am cooking for you, but don't worry, we have a large plate for dessert."

Wow! Though my mind was blown I managed to utter out the words, "I already ate?", with a slight shrug while biting on my pointer finger. He laughed and said, "Good. I didn't cook anyway."

I knew it! I was ALMOST turned off, but things were moving so fast that I had no time for that. He had already picked me up and carried me to the plastic-covered coffee table. He moved like a bank robber escaping with the money bag in hand. He demanded for me to strip naked and lay face-down on the table. I briefly worried the table wouldn't hold my weight, but I obeyed. I did as I was told and got on all fours.

He walked away and came back with a glass jar filled with a brown substance that was too light to be chocolate. He poured the warm thick brown liquid from the top of my neck down the crack of my ass, and his tongue followed as he licked everywhere the syrup went. When he got to my ass, he did not miss a drop and gave special attention to details. I screamed out and caught myself.

He stopped immediately, got very serious and said two words that let me know I was in trouble. "Scream Louder!" Oh, I screamed! He licked faster. The more I screamed, the more he licked.

I pleaded with him and literally begged for a break because I could no longer take it. I felt that I was losing my voice. I needed water. He lifted my body, smacked my ass, and told me to go over to the bed. I was so thirsty but still obliged without hesitation. I jumped on the bed and landed on my stomach. "Flip over," he demanded.

I rolled over and there was the syrup jar.

He kept his eyes on me as he walked over and picked up what I now know as Grade B Maple Syrup (Dark and Robust) in a mason jar. That man held the jar high over my naked body and just stared me down. His look was so serious and intense, though I wasn't afraid, I wondered if Rodrigo was possessed. Inside I burned from anticipation of what he would do next. He didn't make me wait long. Slowly and calculatedly Rodrigo drizzled syrup in an up and down pattern on my lips and kept the flow going. I stuck my tongue out to taste the liquid from the jar. The maple tasted sweet and sticky as it dripped down the side of my cheeks, to my neck, chest and breast. As the syrup dripped down the sides of my body I heard it drop onto the plastic-covered bed. Rodrigo (whom by that point I changed his name mid act to something more fitting- Captain Rod) took time to gather the excess syrup and rubbed it thoroughly on both of my nipples and all over my breast. Then he did a slow pour down my stomach and filled up my belly button. From there, he went down both of my legs to my toes starting at the biggest. Before I could even consider neglect, he whispered in my ear, "I am saving the best for last."

That sent a vibration through my spine and made my pelvic tip upward towards him. He put the jar down and took off his linen pants. He didn't have any underwear on, so as soon as he unzipped his pants, his hard dick freed itself from the fabric and waited like a soldier standing at attention awaiting his next command. By the time his pants hit the floor, he was on top of me like a lion on his prey.

He looked deep into my eyes for an intense moment and just grinded his body against mine. I wanted to reach for him and pull his big dick inside of me, but his stare had me paralyzed. When he decided to release his gaze, he went to work like an artist on his canvas. He retraced his steps and started with my lips. He sucked and licked until all of his syrup work was gone. All that was left was my lonely lips longing for his return. His tongue led him down my neck, to my chest and then my breasts whose nipples were standing at full salute waiting for their turn.

When he arrived at my nipples, he slowed down and took his time. I felt as if my breasts were giving him the nectar of life. He sucked so delicately hard I knew that it was a mastered skill. How could he be so gentle yet so dominant with them? I tried not to think about how this was clearly not his first rodeo as he pulled out new tricks and knew exactly what to do from head to toe. Once he left my breast, his tongue playfully splashed around in my belly button then he kissed and massaged my legs all the way to my toes.

The way I screamed as he sucked my toes sounded as if I was taking the actual 13 inches! When I would try to run off, he pulled me back and sucked harder. He whispered to me, "Mami please don't run from me!" I sighed.

I tried to let him finish, but I truly didn't have any scream left in me. Once he felt his job was complete, he said, "Don't move. I will be right back."

Of course I didn't budge. I could have made my escape, but I was slightly happy to get a break and take a breath from ecstasy. Besides, I was paralyzed from passion. He returned a few minutes later, jarless. I was a little disappointed to not see it when he read my thoughts again and murmured in a low, deep and sexy voice, "No more maple syrup, I need to taste you as is. I missed your taste and smell so much, baby."

From those words alone- break time was over, and I was wet all over again! He started to kiss my inner thighs then went straight for my box.

He licked, ate, sucked, slurped, and wasted nothing. His mouth had become a vacuum sucking up anything that came from me. And the more wetness I produced, the louder the vacuum was.

The sounds from him licking and sucking me all up were mesmerizing. I just melted away. I became one with the plastic. After he licked more than his share and his appetite was filled, it was time to dip all of his rock hard muscle inside of this warm pool that he created.

The first stroke, we both let out a moan of anticipation and remembrance. He fingered and pulled my scalp as he pushed inside as deep as he could go. His eyes were squeezed tightly as his tongue worked overtime from penetrating my mouth to sucking the remaining syrup off of my face. When he could no longer hold on to the moment, he released a roar so loud I was sure that he woke up everyone in the building.

We laid there in silence, sticky, sweaty, with hearts beating wildly. Our mouths wide open from shock as we stared at the ceiling wondering if what had just taken place really happened. For the first time since I arrived I looked out the window. I saw a glimpse of the sun peeking over the clouds. I looked over at him and saw that he was looking at me. He smiled, grabbed my hand, kissed it then dozed off. I smiled, looked around his loft and then my eyes landed on his empty kitchen.

It was at that moment, the spell was over, and I was able to release myself. This man was too much and not enough at the same time.

After he dozed off to sleep, I quietly gathered my belongings (including the jar of syrup) and snuck my sticky ass out without a peep. On my way home, I called the phone company and requested a phone number change. Sometimes, a girl has to know when a situation is not healthy. Too much of him would be a safety hazard. The only thing that I decided to keep from that situation was the maple.

Maple is my name. And after experiencing this story, I guarantee you that you won't look at syrup the same.

# II. *Confession*

Someday, my prince will come.

But…

until then…

I will appreciate the frogs and take full advantage of their tongue capabilities.

— LadyLovingWaiting

# Nobody's Bitch

I am not a bitch.

I am a man in total connection with my gate. A gatekeeper.

A man that is comfortable enough in himself and

one who is able and willing to express my deepest emotions and desires.

I will share a secret with you…

I am a man that enjoys being dominated.

Spank me, tell me what to do, and punish me if I don't do it to your liking.

I am a man that at times yearns to be held at night.

I may even get upset and throw a tantrum when I don't get it right —
but no less a man.

I am a man that enjoys getting stimulated anally even if it's only annually.

Don't get nervous, I am just open to exploring my sexuality.

Do I not seem masculine enough because tonight you can't touch me, I only want to lick your pussy?

Does it confuse you that I don't want any penis play tonight, but I may want to fuck you right in the morning?

Believe it or not, this man is not always horny for the physical. Perhaps visual stimulation will do.

As a man, I feel the constant need to defend my title of manhood and not fully express my desires though I know, I am a man despite where my sexual mind goes.

Understand

I am every man

All of the labels and stigma thrown everywhere, it will do you injustice to put me in your box.

…. Unless I want to be in there.

— a Manly Man

# III. *Confession*

The sex last night had me smoking a cigarette on my back porch wearing only a fur coat and a pair of thigh highs.

#ididntsmokebeforelastnight

# Those Toes

When I met her,

The attraction was exceptionally strong

She was exotic beautiful, and sweet

I could not find anything wrong

there was something about her,

apart from her beautiful glow

It was her fishnet stockings

covering those pretty red toes


That woman brought me to my knees

Embarrassingly quick

When she strutted over to her pedestal

Lifted her right foot and

Didn't ask but demanded with one word:

Lick!


I took her toes and licked them

Then rubbed them on my face

I knew right then this woman

Could never be replaced.

She cupped her feet together and

I put my cock in between

I didn't realize how much she'd oiled them
Until I heard myself scream

My masculinity was gone

And manhood put to the test

I am in love with her feet

they have 100 percent of my interest

I cleaned up her feet then decided to

Give her toes individual attention

Then I put all five in my mouth

And sucked with intention

I couldn't believe how good they made me feel

those toes had me ready to seal the deal

I was convinced that toes are nutritious

if not, they were definitely delicious

Those magnificent toes

have the power to heal my woes

I will follow them…her, wherever she goes

# IV. *Confession*

Fishnet Stockings

Satin Thong

Leather Corset

Tasty Tongue =

Everything I had for Breakfast

— Happy Meal

# Dick Fetish?

I have a dick fetish...I think

I love cock.

I appreciate my Mr. Johnsons in various shapes, sizes, and colors.

Hot dogs are my favorite food.

I love having to open my mouth as wide as I can to fit the thick piece of meat inside of my mouth.

I like my cucumbers like I like my sausage — as big and long as I can find them.

I spend an abnormal amount of time finding just the right sizes.

My favorite TOOL is the HAMMER for its pounding abilities.

I can't help but admire how it dominates the nails that lie vulnerable in its scope.

I also enjoy being pounded by various types of hammers. Recently, after sampling various hardware stores I've self-analyzed and concluded:

One size hammer in my toolbox does not satisfy every job!

Something else about my fetish is, I tend to suck on 3 Super Blow Pops a day.

Sucking one blow pop after the other until my jaw literally hurts.

It's something about sucking hard on a sweet stick that I have full control over.

I can move the candy around in my mouth and stick it down as deep as I want — which is normally until I gag for kicks...and practice.

I grab knobs and turn them slowly with extra attention and grip- then I release it slowly.

When I eat pickles, whether they are big juicy dills or a little gherkin, I am sure to do it slow because I like when the juice drips down my chin.

Ordering me a donut? You may have already guessed; I

want a cream-filled Long John, but I will suck up the

jelly too.

Keep the Ding

I'll take the Dong

I prefer my joysticks long

I don't care for Vera as much as I do Wang.

Yes! I'd love for you and your

Plonker to show me a few things

I recently did some firing so

I am in the process of hiring

A whole new staff

What is the description you ask?

I am seeking a lender

to bring in a member

that specializes in the center.

Interested?

Apply Inside

# Tongue Tied

The naughty side of me loves
when he comes home from work stressed.
He yells from the front door for
me to go and get undressed.

I oblige.

He comes into the room and tells me
to assume my position.
I'm nervous but excited to help
relieve his tension.
He looks at me as he aggressively
removes his tie.
I see the fire turned passion
in his eye.
He goes to the closet and
…. oh my!
I think he's getting more
I was right!
He comes back holding four.

He says, "You've been a naughty girl.

I'm going to punish you,

And I'm afraid one

one tie just won't do."

He begins by tying both of

my hands to my leg.

My body starts to heat up

as I scream and I beg.


He reminds me of what happened last time

and

how long it's been

Once I'm all tied up

The games begin.

He squeezes my cheeks and bites my lips "You've been daddy's bad girl!"

He rubs down my body and pinches my nips.

I shriek in painful pleasure

He covers my mouth and tells me don't

let out a sound again

Or he promises the sex torture will never end.

I bite my own lip

He puts his face between my legs and

proceeds to finger and lick

-Greedily

As if he skipped breakfast, lunch, AND dinner for weeks

The over pour of pleasure takes away my power

My sink sprung a leak

I begged and pleaded for him to STOP

Pleeeeeease!

No, don't stop! Keep going— Ok, please stop

I can't... Yes, just a little more

Clutching whatever I can grab

The pillows fall to the floor.

But he doesn't hear me.

In my bonded position, I can't stop him no matter how hard I tried,

He pleasure tortures me with his whole tongue;

I swear I didn't realize it was so wide

He doesn't ask me if I like it

He trusted my moans to be his guide

Tongue torture at its finest he has me tongue-tied.

I had become victim to his game

and I never would have bet

after his tongue seizure inside of me

The surprise was

the true torture, hadn't begun yet.

He wanted me quiet

taking his torture silent

Out a noise I let

his demands were not met

he walked away, and

left me lying there,

throbbing, tied up and

soaking wet.

— Fuck.

# V. Confession

Crawl to me

Get yo sexy ass on the floor

and crawl.

Yeah! Just like that.. crawl

across the floor to me…

— Obey

# Punish Me

"Shut up and sit down!" Madame Anigav demanded.

She didn't want to hear my excuses on why I was late.

I quickly sat in my chair.

She put her book down and slowly walked over with my collar.

"What are you doing in that chair? Get your late ass on the floor where you belong."

Oh, *I'm in trouble now*, I thought.

"Yes, Madam." I happily got on the floor.

"Put this on." She said with disgust.

She threw my collar at me, and I felt slightly disappointed that she didn't want to put it on me herself. As I put the collar on and handed her my leash I saw the others watching me. She connected the leash to my collar and began to walk me around the room. I crawled shamefully behind her diamond-studded heels.

She suddenly stopped and turned around. She lifted her leg and pressed her stiletto against my chest and forced me to my back. As I lied down she firmly said, "Open your mouth"! I opened wide, and she spat her sweet saliva inside and told me not to swallow. I obeyed. She knelt down and sat on my face and gave me a golden shower. "Now swallow!" she demanded as she tried to drown me with her urine. I moved my head side to side wanting to oblige while also having the need to breathe. Once she had her fun she stood up, yanked on my leash and demanded that I get back into position. She walked over to a shelf, grabbed a towel and threw it at me. "Clean yourself up"! I wiped away what I could and returned to my position. While on all fours I saw her reach for her paddle. She wasn't done with me. She slapped the paddle against her hand and asked, "You have been a VERY BAD BOY, haven't you?"

"Yes, Madam Ani-" POW! She spanked me.

"Have you been a bad boy?"

"Yes, Ani-"POW! Another hit.

"Say it faster!"

"Yes, Madame Anigav! I have been bad!" I said it so fast I only hoped that I got it right.

She was pleased. "Now, that's a good boy," she said with a smile of satisfaction. She went back to the front of the class, grabbed her book and continued instruction.

# The Hunted

*Pull over and fuck me!*

Why do you have to be so vulgar?

*Pull over and have sex with me!*

I don't respond..

*Baby, pull over and let me love on you.*

Don't patronize me.

*But I -*

Babe, not now, we will be there soon.

*Ok baby, how about you pull over and just give me a hug?*

I look over at her and can't help but smile.
She actually made one of *my* begging faces.
"Oh really? So, you are going to give me that old line?"
I can't help but to fall for it-especially
When she leaned in and whispered,

*"Only 5 seconds"*

It was incredibly sexy.

I pulled the truck over to give her a hug.

She convinced me to get out and walk over to her side of the truck. She opened the door with a sneaky grin hugged me, wrapped her legs around my waist tightly

then whispered in my ear,

*"Why don't you just stick the tip in?"*

I chuckled. "Only the tip? Now you know that's going to make you crazy. Just be honest"

*"Ok, ok, 5 strokes? Just Three..."*

"Only three? " DAMN, she got me.

She giggled but then tried to look serious.

I lifted up her dress and found myself desiring her badly.

This woman!

She was not wearing any panties and was already wet.

I felt set up.

I was under her spell

3 strokes turned into 5,

5 turned into 15

I gave in and lost count.

She stared at me the entire time.

Her deep intense look made me close my eyes in hopes of keeping my emotions together.

When she moaned that she was cumming, I released with her. .

Once my thoughts were clear again I looked at her with disbelief and violation.

"I feel plotted on," I said in vulnerability.

She replied, *"As you should"*

She kissed my forehead,

turned into her seat, laid back

and went to sleep for the rest of the drive.

# Open Wide

When you say that you are "wide open"

Do you mean — Open? Open?

Like, wide open as in, I'm ok with not being his main because I just want to be in the line up-open?

Wide-open, as in, I know she's creeping behind my back,

but I'll take her back again- open.


Sometimes I wonder if I'm wide open or maybe, I'm just coping.

Either way I am hoping.

that there is a good side to this so-called wide-open

besides a passion so deep, in words it can't be spoken.


#Used

# Two + One = Zero

I have a confession and it's not easy but there's nothing like honesty on your worst day.

I really didn't want to even muster up the energy nor courage to get dressed and face the world
but I needed to get out of the house. I jumped up, threw on my wool coat and a green scarf large enough to hide in.

What I wore underneath the coat was not worth mentioning

I had the appearance of a person that didn't want to talk to anyone.

I decided to take Las Vegas Blvd and drive down the strip. I didn't want to go home so I stopped at my breakfast spot, The Peppermill. I normally get the same order but today I wasn't hungry at all. I started to question why I was even there but I needed to get away from the crime scene.

I walked inside and felt like everyone looked up as if I had a dramatic entrance. It seemed like they all judged me for my careless decision.

When I walked up to the hostess stand, I could tell she was taken aback by what stood in front of her.

"I'm not feeling well," I felt compelled to say to the stranger. "Ma'am...you look...great."

Lie.

I didn't need that right now.

I may have looked like I needed lies right then, but I didn't.

After the night I had all I needed was the truth and caffeine to get me through this day.

The threesome from last night had me dazed and confused.

Standing directly in the middle of right and w-h-a-t t-h-e-f-u-c-k?

Flashes of my best friend moaning in passion mixed with sights of my husband's cock stroking her from behind kept interrupting my thoughts. "Not shitting where you eat" has never meant more to me than it does right now. Buyers remorse has set in and now hindsight is crystal clear. I felt nauseous.

I admit that I wasn't innocent, after all, I was the mastermind but damn! It did not take much convincing. I was the one who actually thought it was a good idea to share an intimate experience with two of my favorite people. I never considered how difficult it would be to look at her the same after she licked and sucked on my clitoris until I begged for her to stop. Or the feeling of watching my husband look at her with amazement, as she teased his balls with her tongue. Watching the focus he put in his waist as he wound his hips and thrusted every inch of MY DICK inside of her…how could I trust the two of them together alone again?

My coffee order interrupted my insecure reality. I saw the waitress slip a note into the napkins with my cup. I was too caught up in the sex filled disaster of my night before to even care.

As I sat at the counter looking out the window, I saw a piece of paper fly from a girl's open purse, reminding me of the note placed near my cup.

I pulled the piece of paper out and unfolded its message. My first laugh of the day came from blunt honesty. Scrawled across the paper was, "You look like shit, go home and start over."

# Secretly Seeking

I am shy but I have A LOT of freaky thoughts running around my head,

as you walk by, I picture playing them out on you in my bed.

You always look right over me, As I look right through you Oooooooh

You so underestimate me as the sexual being that I am! Because in a public space, I may be shy but

In private I guarantee I can keep every part of you at attention,

But first thing first: Hello

# Our Bodies

Our bodies are like magnets

When we are around each other

The inner G is steaming hot

We can't control ourselves

There is a NEED for touching

With each glance, we become more addicted

both of us, enjoying the spell

Fully surrendering never

Felt

So

Free.

# VI. *Confession*

He had the best dick in the world-No, in the universe—

Scratch that, the best dick EVER!

Until we broke up.

Then his dick turned into the shriveled tool that it always was.

Yes, I still want...ed it.

— Whipped

# VII. *Confession*

It was at this intense moment when I decided to let go…

I no longer cared about what crazy faces I was making

or how bad my hair was going to look after. I was aware

that my makeup was no longer fresh and there was a

risk that nothing would be the same again, but I did it

anyway.

I let go.

And when I did, the most amazing feeling allowed all of my senses to perform a vertical dance throughout my body and opened up my sacral chakra to liberate my juices. The orgasmic pleasures rolled through my hips like aftershocks from a 9.0 earthquake. My body was so wet, giving in to that moment allowed me to experience my first orgasmic rain dance.

# Confused

I heard the moans when I walked through the door. A flash of confusion, anger, and passion all in one was overwhelming. I ran upstairs and burst through our bedroom door. My purse dropped. She was stroking his dick as he fingered her while eating her pussy. The way he was so, so...into it. I hadn't seen him enjoy anything like that — especially me.

You'd have thought I'd been starving the man. Her eyes were closed as she enjoyed being the recipient of such pleasure.

A tear fell down my eye slowly. When it got to my chin, it stopped. It was as if it had paused to glance at its purpose. Then that tear slowly fell. Once it hit the ground, it made the loudest sound. Loud enough that the objects of my heartbreak stopped and for the first time realized my presence.

They stared with disbelief anticipating my reaction. I debated which weapon to seize, what octave to yell but all I could mutter out my clenched teeth was,

"I thought you didn't like a bush."

# VIII. *Confession*

I have heard the legend of the Big King Dick That rounds rears and rids acne quick

I'm looking for the legend hiding among average men

To suck him into submission

And let him plow this land

The thickest in the nation

Known to make you cum again and again.

I am ready to receive the first installation to ensure the legend never ends.

# Black Satin

I love satin sheets. Black satin to be exact. He brought me into the room and told me to get naked. Slowly, I began to remove my skirt, he impatiently pushed me hard onto the bed and I fell down on my back. He looked at me with a serious face and demanded, "dance for me". I began slowly dancing while still lying down. I slid slowly to the left then slowly back to the right. I began spreading my legs open and closed. Whether I am pleasing myself or allowing the pleasure of someone to please me the satin sheets are forgiving. I take my satin sheets, roll them up and put them on my clitoris. I rock my pelvic back and forth on the satin fabric. They tease my sense of touch. I love to roll over on my stomach and let the tip of my nipples rub against the smooth texture. On a cold day they shock my skin and I need some sort of friction to stay warm. These satin sheets are something that I want to share with you.

Will you cum?

# Sexual Opponent

I think that I will never see

a person that can outlast me

A dick so strong

A pussy so wet

Still searching but

Have never met

Sex without the

Restrictions of time

Bodies afraid to rest

Putting endurance to the test

Challenging the passion

Pushing the mind

I think that I will never see

A sex partner that shares

My mentality

# *Kats got your tongue…*

I'm walking down the beach in Isla Verde, or should I say, prancing. My sun dress is no accident because it accentuates this body. This is my favorite dress to wear on the beach because it dances with the waves. I have my sandals in one hand and a bottle of water to cool me down in the other. Let's just call it what it is, I am putting on an all-out show for whoever is watching, and I have all of their attention. I am an implanted island girl. I moved to the island 3 decades ago when I was in grade school so this is the home that I know. As I prance I hear a faint voice traveling over the sounds from the ocean yell my name, "Kat! Kat!" but I continue to stroll. I know exactly who the voice belongs to:

Leslie. The sexiest Puerto Rican on the island, and he out of all people has to be my neighbor. I slow down just enough so that he can catch up but without looking back.

"Kat! Didn't you hear me calling you? That is your name isn't it?" he asks.

"You should know since you hand-deliver my mail every day…" I said it with slight annoyance, but I didn't mean it.

"First of all, let's get it straight — your mail was delivered to MY box, and I decided to do you a favor. But hey, no problem, I don't mind sending it back…" he teased.

"No, no, thank you." I got myself together right away.

"That's what I'm talking about," he says with a cocky grin that immediately makes me wonder how good in bed he is. At that moment he became my newest mission.

I look at him and ask, "Can I buy you a drink?"

Startled, he replied, "Tonight? Tomorrow? You caught me off guard."

"Well, you are at least 21, right?"

He laughs and nods his head. "I am 22. Actually, I will be 23 in 4 months."

"Mmmm, that's cute. I was thinking more like having a drink now."

"Now?" He tenses up.

"Yes, you did just chase me down the beach. You don't seem too busy so...."

"Ok cool. I...will take you up on that...but I didn't chase you, ok? I followed you with a purpose."

"Well, now you've caught me, what are you going to do to me...I mean, with me?"

He laughs again and shakes his head. He was about to say something but instead just shook his finger at me and smiled.

I smile back. We walk to the Blu Guayaba in silence. I don't think he knew what to say to me. I broke the ice when we sat at the bar by ordering shots right away. You know, to ease the tension.

The third shot is when the communication starts flowing freely. He tells me his passions, and I listen and believe in his dreams with him. By the fifth shot, we are up dancing to Afrobeats. He dances down low, and I sway my hips to the ground to meet him. We then come back up grinding our bodies together. We dirty danced for a bit before I asked him to escort me to the bathroom to help me unzip my dress.

When we got inside the restroom he began to look for the zipper in the back when I spun around and kissed him deeply.

He grabs the back of my neck with one hand and body with the other so tightly and possessively I moan with ecstasy and passion. I open his mouth with my hands and try to suck his tongue out — he returns the gesture. He then bends me over the sink and pulls my dress up and slides his stiff dick inside my super wet pussy.

We stare at each other in the mirror as he pumps me hard with rhythmic thrusts.

As he grabs my hair he questions, "Kat, Kat, what's my name? What's my name, baby… Kat?"

As I stare into his eyes I see the chocolate brown circles light up with fire as the sun hits them. His smooth dark skin and big sexy smile just seem like a present ready to be opened.

"Kat, Kat?" his voice sounds concerned. The bathroom scene fades, and I hear the ocean waves again. I laugh out loud.

"What is it?" I ask. He stops walking to wait for a response. "Is it something that I said?"

At that very moment, I realized that I hadn't heard anything that he said at all. "Do you prefer that I change the subject? It seems like I've completely lost your attention." He was disappointed. With a grin I confirm, "No, no you have my attention. I was just thinking maybe we should go have a drink at the Blu Guayaba?"

# VIIII. *Confession*

I decided not to ask him how he became a better lover during our absence, but to accept it and take it as the blessing that it was.

— Wet and Unbothered

# Addiction

Addict-Shon

A Dick Shon

A dick named shon

For him, I would do things. The type of things that I never thought I would do. How could I love something more than myself? Easy — he was firm, dependable, strong, and ALWAYS came through.

The better question is...how could I not? For him, I made the wrong decisions willfully

To stay in his good grace,

I allowed the unspeakable but only because I had nothing to say

He put the words inside of my mouth

My vocabulary became involuntary

He released emotions from my body that awoke sleeping parts of my soul

that I didn't realize existed.

He showed me that there are levels

to this sex shit

I have never felt so sexy,

so free, so...wanted.

He taught me a whole new love.

I called him the alchemist.

He was POWERFUL.

He was the head of many soldiers and commanded with such authoritative force, it wasn't a question of "Will I obey?" it was only a matter of "When?"

We imprinted on each other each other

and felt that our connection would never end.

But it did.

I eventually realized that yes, the dick was firm, dependable, strong, and always came through but

it sucks when the person it's attached to depreciates his value.

It was a strong A.Dick.Shon

# *The days that lead to Sunday*

Dante' came over Monday as frustrated as can be. He found out that he was getting laid off after dedicating 10 years to his company. That decision had blindsided him and he felt disgusted with himself for not seeing the signs of the chopping block being near. I was at a loss for words. Lending an ear was what he needed from me and in the end, worked in my favor. From my experience words won't help much in a situation like this anyway. I remained silent and allowed him to vent as long as he needed. While I was in no position to hire him full time, I felt that I was able to use his qualifications for a temporary project. What I found most attractive about Dante' was that he was a hard worker. No one could take that from him. Every inch of his body reflected his work ethic. His serious eyebrows. The eyelashes that tirelessly danced around fanning the most beautiful gray eyes. Those sincere eyes that projected his intense stare reflected his soul. His strong jawbone used all of its strength when he clenched his jaw lifting something heavy or when they exposed his dimples.

His specialty was in precision. He found the area that needed attention and worked on it until the job was completed to your satisfaction. That was exactly the kind of help that I was looking for. I hired him on the spot.

He was the best driller, and you should know that drilling is not for the weak. But Dante's back was built for labor- intensive work. After I listened to his unfortunate story, I called him to my office to show him the project that I needed his help with.

He jumped at the opportunity. He started from the ground up and I found his work to be extremely thorough and efficient. That is why I prefer to use his services on Mondays, which are my most stressful days. Mr. Dante has mastered the art of being in and out without missing a spot so I will continue to keep him employed for now. Afterall, I am a businesswoman, and I don't mind paying for convenience.

Tuesday, I went to puff and paint for the 5th time. I go even though I don't like painting. I actually despise it. So, what keeps me paying $40 for a canvas I throw away after each class? A sexy ass instructor named Donovan-but I call him Donny. He doesn't know that I call him Donny yet, but I was hoping that after class I could express my gratitude for his sexual qualities that keep me cumming back.

He has to be aware of the vibe he is putting out there. very masculine… very open… very artistic… very…fuckable. He made me love long hair on a masculine physique and I could only imagine all of the other creative things he could make me do. During class I convinced him to allow me to stay after for a private lesson to brush up on my technique. He agreed. To my surprise he turned my body into a canvas, and I was not disappointed at all with his masterpiece. He started with a paint brush on my body and by the end we were huffing and puffing completely covered in paint. I never paid for that class again.

Wednesday I decided to take it easy and call over my Netflix and Chill. Robbie is my white boy who has an eating disorder that I enjoy taking advantage of. He has an eat black pussy fetish so I let him have at it and allow him to dine until closing while I watch my favorite flick.

He loves to rub oil all over my body and bite my ass before he gets to work. Like clockwork, when his tongue gets tired he curls up to me, sucks my breast then falls asleep. I keep him around to get me over the hump days.

Thursday was my Personal Chef's day. I love a man that can cook and when I tell you David brought the beef...He was USDA certified baby. He loved to cook but loved to feed me even more. He would stuff me with food for hours. He likes to feed me a lot. I know that we are going to eat the best food until we fall asleep every time. The one thing that changes is what he wakes me up to. Most times I wake up to him fingering or pounding my ass from the back. He prefers to cum this way. Afterwards we feast all over again.

He certainly keeps my cravings full for the almost end of week vibe.

Fridays I set a fire that burns only for my fireman Antonio. After fighting fires all day, he cums here to be my hero and saves me from my energy drained week. He brings his large hose, and it turns me into a siren. Antonio sparks my weekend flame. My sexual soulmate the Fireman.

Saturday I hung out with my hippie yogi, Anderson. I sacrifice meat for a whole day to be in his pure presence. Oh, did I mention that he is a vegan too? I don't know what it is but it seems that most yogis that I fuck are vegan. I guess conscious eating just comes with the package. When I arrived at his house he told me to undress. He blindfolded me and led me to his tub that he had filled with dozens of rose petals. He bathed me in water scented with Lavender oil and guided me through Kegel exercises while massaging my breast. He played relaxing music and at some point maybe a flute? I don't know, I was dozing off. This was just the pampering that I needed after my busy week. At some point I was bent over in the tub giving Anderson the best head that I had to give. I can't get enough of his taste. Maybe there is something to his healthy diet because his sperm tastes organic, and I swear that it cleared up an acne breakout that I had once. I have to keep Andy around. He is always teaching and keeps me hydrated.

Sunday I stopped by my favorite coffee shop super early before heading to repent my past week's shenanigans. As I sat drinking my rose latte, I checked my calendar and began planning my upcoming week. As I take another sip, I look up and spot a sexy pair of eyes staring at me. The mask hid most of his face but from his nice tie, tailored suit, clean Stacy Adam shoes and statement piece socks I didn't need to see more to know that this man was *somebody*. The size of his hands as he turned his newspaper turned me curiously naughty on top of my spontaneous personality. I made a bold move and wrote on a napkin *"meet me in the bathroom"*, folded it up neatly and dropped it off at his table. I then proceeded to my new temporary office. As I waited to see how bold *he was,* I reminisced on how classy his scent was when I walked by. I also decided at that moment that I did not want to see his whole face nor him to see mine because this was going to be a true wildcard one day stand. I waited 4 min and when I decided this may be a little crazy and to save my wildcard for another rainy day I opened the door and there he was. He started talking, "I didn't know if I should knock…"

Before he spoke enough words to turn me off I pulled him inside of the bathroom by his tie. Once inside I said 4 words "keep your mask on".

I knew the importance of those words, but I could never have realized the imperativeness of them at the time to the entire situation. At first I was excited by the mere thought of inviting a masked stranger to the bathroom. I honestly had no intentions outside of a lot of groping and teasing. The encounter started to almost feel too easy because of the soft almost familiar look in his sexy eyes . The groping didn't go on for long because one scan of my body and my Sunday dress was up and around my hips. I had already slid my panties in my purse - you know for teasing purposes. He lifted me on the bathroom sink and when he began to pleasure my body I felt like this man loved me.

Yes somehow I had some accidental love making stranger sex on Sunday morning. As if this wasn't sinning enough, little did I know there were more sins to come in the powder room of my favorite coffee shop. When he decided to turn me over it got to the point that he was stroking in and out so deeply that he had to cover my mouth to contain the shrieks of taking it all in. I broke the rule. I had to see the face of this heavyweight. I needed to know exactly who was responsible for the pleasure I had sought out for so long. I turned and looked back as much as I could to not interrupt the flow. His eyes were squeezed closed with amazement of just how he came about experiencing this Sunday Morning special.

That detail added more wetness to the situation. As my breast bounced and jiggled with satisfaction, they filled my mystery lover's hands and labeled them occupied. During my slow winding motion (hooks them every time) I reached back to grab his face but accidentally pulled his mask down a bit. With the speed of lighting I quickly pulled the face cover back up before he even noticed. Maybe it was the shock in my eyes or the realization of the situation that made him slow down but the passion left his eyes and he abruptly stopped. With no words I watched my Pastor as he picked up his pants from around his ankle and returned to decency.

Pastor Johnson looked at me, shook my hand, and walked out. I could not help but to wonder if he knew it was me all along.

Well, needless to say, I skipped church that Sunday... but I will be present the next.

# Twin flames

He walked up on me

and approached

me from behind

I looked over at my husband

but he didn't seem to mind

Though he was entwined with

his own little find.

# Be careful of what you ask

I admit that I was a little hurt when she asked

if I perform this on every woman that I slept with.

How dare she mutter that doubt-

-that open curiosity.

Could the question wait?

Do I lick ass on the first date?

Only if the situation requires that

I eat the entire plate.

Sushi connoisseurs can relate

You get charged extra if you leave

edible items behind.

Yes, I'd rather get behind the situation

So, on occasion

I prefer buffets to dine

# *Here kitty kitty*

This pussy reads and this pussy feeds

Off the Inner G that plants the seeds

This pussy leads this pussy needs

You to purr at this kitty to enter the speakeasy

Something else that this pussy needs is

attention that matches her Inner G please

This kitty's blunt all this kitty wants

is to be pleasured the best

without needing rest

passion for passion

she stands to the test.

# *Confession* XXX

One night after passion reintroduced itself to me, I lied there staring at the ceiling. How had my lover disappeared into the cold night over 46 minutes ago yet my legs were still shaking. There was so much wetness between my legs my fingers were intimidated to feel it. My nipples were on full alert searching for a signal to send out a message to whomever had done this to my body to return A.S.A.P.

As I lay looking at the ceiling I had deep thoughts AND answers. The most profound of them was how he managed to release 7 orgasms from me in 11 minutes. What happened differently? Was it my sheets? The store clerk told me that I wouldn't regret the purchase. In hindsight I dismissed her sinister smile since it was our first encounter, but did she understand the power of touch and intimacy? Maybe that's too deep to consider but that's what I'm concluding. That's where the sex had me mentally and emotionally. I had the time to stare at this ceiling of mine.

Scenes of my body sliding across my smooth black satin sheets. The strokes went so deep as my body slid with the motions. It was like a waterbed with no water. We made love on a black satin ocean. After lying staring at the ceiling for 38 minutes I answered myself on why on October 10, 2020 in the midst of a pandemic I allowed myself to have seven orgasms? That's right, seven is what I said.

It's because I decided to let go. At first I was given permission with the words "let go" whispered in my ear. My body immediately complied and relaxed. Out slid the first O. When the second "let go" came into my ear it was with more of an authoritative tone and that really turned me on, so the second orgasm came easy. The third orgasm was so strong my entire body trembled. And to think I was okay with bragging to my friends about my three. I would soon find out that it was all pregame to me having over a dozen orgasms in less than 12 minutes. By the time the fourth orgasm released itself I was getting the hang of it. They started to happen from the smallest touch and facial expressions. I became one with the orgasm and multiplied myself.

# Fingers Lie

He had small hands but his middle finger was long

So I was optimistic but

I was wrong

I was wrong.

# *Sharing size*

Be confident and don't mind lending this cock. After all it is sharing size. Don't you dare consider it cheating because there is an art to pleasing. It requires dedication and time. There is a commitment that I am willing to make to you: As long as you continue to throw it back, I will continue to bring it back with satisfaction guaranteed.

# Toxic Greatness

He loves to torture me by inflicting pleasure with pain. The more pain he causes, the more he enjoys it. This particular night he has the room lit with candles. I smile though I know that he's not nice enough to be romantic. I smile because I know how he thinks. It's the hot wax from the candles that he wants to pour all over my body and make me scream. I hide my nervousness. In moments like this I find pleasure in the anticipation, followed by the pain of the hot wax, the pulling of my hair and the hard thrusts of his dick. He puts my body on a sexual rollercoaster of emotions with excitement, fear and hesitancy. I get over my fears and take my clothes off. Of course I let him do it. I will do anything that he asks of me. When I scream I can see the fire glow in his eyes. His lust filled touch burns with desire. I have to plead with him to have mercy but it falls on deaf ears. He just menacingly stares at my reaction as he gets closer and closer to a climax. This intense power-driven stare is the most emotion that I can get from him. Most times I can't tell what he's thinking because his expressions are so serious and that turns me on. I can feel his hate when he loves me at these moments. I don't want him to stop so bad. You read that right. Tortured with lust is a different kind of orgasm. I want him to stop as much as I need him to continue. How can I crave for him to hurt me so?

#latoxica

# Speak up

I have something else to say

So come closer I dare you

Do you like what I'm saying

I hope my boldness doesn't scare you

These words I speak are trying to

prepare you

Don't be offended because tonight

I want to share you

Don't tense up, it's the

good kind of bad

Tonight will be the best group sex

that you ever had

#groupworship

# Getting back on the saddle

Fooling around with Jack last night, I couldn't help but regret not taking my horseback riding lessons more seriously as a child. I gave up riding at the barn at the age of 16 but was reintroduced to the art of riding a stallion last night! Perhaps if I were more of a trained rider, it would have reflected in my performance. I would have been confident with taking control and taught the dick how to respect me. Instead I nervously straddled him while staring down into his eyes begging for him to take over. Had I used his shirt for my reins and his lap as my saddle…up and down, up and down remembering that my thighs trained for this three days a week for five years- I would have blown his mind. Instead I forced him to do the work, allowing him to tightly hold on to my hips and guide my body. When he took control, he pushed his way inside of me until he could go no further. I felt every inch of him. I didn't necessarily want him that deep, but it was no longer up to me. I had relinquished my rights by this time. He knew it before I did and pumped his pelvic with full force as if he was aiming for my heart. All I could do was just hold on for the ride and try my hardest not to fall off. When a rare intermission was taken, I caught a glimpse of his human side taking a drink of water. The muscles in his back flexed with every motion as if he was a warrior. He soon proved to me that he was just that. This was not the work of an average man. I couldn't help but be disappointed in my performance. I could have had a more aggressive response to the whole ordeal like bouncing back, giving positive reinforcement with each pump and maybe giving attention to his balls. I could have given him more action than just squeezing his chest and making the oooh face and holding in all of my moans.

As I sat and rated myself the lowest score I could have possibly received, something happened. I decided that I wasn't going to allow my lack of sexual expression and participation tonight to make me feel like a complete failure. I remembered something that I could take away from my horseback riding lessons and apply to the situation. I climbed back on the saddle, sat up- got my posture together and broke that stallion with no stirrups.

# *Quickie*

A little quick poetry
about a guy,
We'll call him
"T"
I would have fucked him
for free
but then he offered
me money
I fucked him that time
then twice more
two times
quickly turned in
to four
The moment that really hit me
to the core
was the moment I realized that
I turned into a whore
It wasn't a problem before
until I left my boyfriend
when he refused
to leave money
on the drawer.

# Let's talk nasty----Performance Sex
## Noir Merida, MX
## March 26 2022

Tell me exactly what you want,

no need to be classy.

Do you want to fuck me?

I want to fuck you.

and when we fuck

Remember

this is your thing

do what you want to do

Fuck me now!

No…

Will you fuck me please?

I want to be able to speak freely

I need my thoughts to feel at ease

Tell me exactly what you want

I aim to please

Tonight I'll speak boldly and

talk sexy with no tease.

Tell me your demands

in my ear

Speak as hard or softly

as you feel

Speak without fear

Speak to me nasty

I want to hear

How it feels to be inside of me.

I want you to explain the tear.

I want you to speak to me nasty and

Understand that classy

means ABSOLUTELY nothing right now!

The words I may say

may sound foul

-there's a reason

I'm ready

to talk

Nasty

… to you

and

Say all the freaky shit

that's running around my mind

I honestly don't know

the freaky shit

you will find

The things that I'm thinking are Nasty

and you may think

are behind…ME

but there not

Actually check the rear

and you will find one of my spots


Look, Let's Talk Nasty

I want to be head of your class

Knees ashy

I'm being vulnerable right now

not my normal

nothing classy


Let's pleeease talk Nasty

DAMMIT!

Take this dick

Add 1 more finger

Pull my hair-

I enjoy the pain

Talk to me nasty baby,

Give me a new name

Tonight oral play with me

let's play the word game

Orgasms for a woman is mental

starts in our brain

So speak to my body with words that

keeps my head entertained


Let's talk Nasty and

I don't mean that soft porn shit either

Talk to me nasty Daddy

… or Mami

I want to hear what you have to say

I'm not listening for the words

I want to hear your inner jay (energy)

I want to use my lungs

because of your tongue

Let's add in verbal fun

Let's talk nasty

Let's talk nasty

Let's talk nasty

# *The Sex Last Night*

The sex last night

Made me feel good

Had me cum right

Changed my mentality

Inspired who I want to be

The Sex Last Night

was motivating me

to put it at the least

No words can describe

the best sex

that I ever fathomed

I vote it best thrill ride

The Sex Last Night

The Sex Last Night

Was so damn good I

have to say it twice

The sex was so good

I needed to say it thrice

Time after time

my legs shook

Toes stayed intertwined

Had to turn and see what was

going on behind

The sex looked so good

had to say it a fourth time

The sex last night was so

insane

the way

it made me scream names

The Sex Last Night

Fixed my postured

had me sit upright

Will the next contestant

up tonight

Make me forget

about the sex last night?

# You are not fucking me enough

You are NOT fucking

me enough

You know, not grabbing my ass

and touching me enough

I need to feel wanted

I need to know my dick

is there

I'm a very sexual wombman

I need to know that you care

Great conversation is good but

12 play is on my mind

I want you

holding my waist

while I look back at you

hitting it from behind

I love my man

I'm so turned on by you

but I want you and

I need for you

to want me too.

# My name is - - - - Performance El Remate Merida, MX April 2 2023

My name is Assata

and I write naughty

I'm here to read tonight

to make you want to go home and

fuck somebody

…. even if it's yourself

Don't look at me like that

You came here

so take these words and put

the modesty on the shelf

Tonight I want your mind open-

Treat Yo self


Now you don't have to

necessarily go home

but there's no fucking up in here

and while we're on the topic of

fucking something up

tell me

How do you like it

commandeered?

Wild, rough

Or do you prefer this flavor

… whispered in your ear?

-Do you like how I came from the rear

Speaking of rear let me back

this thang up

and rewind

Grab it, Bend it over

and lick it from behind.

I am Assata

I'm referred to as Queen

Because I can walk into a room

and dominate that thing

Are you wondering if I'm talking

figurative, literal or sexually

I'm a girl that likes options

So assume all 3

I am an Author that publishes

What you won't say but

are thinking

Don't be shy tonight

Release those freaky feelings

My fetish is I'm a watcher

tonight I'm watching

I like to see the reaction

my naughty wordplay brings

Again I am Queen

Telly invited me here tonight

to add naughtiness to the scene

I'm here for the sexual healing

… and EVERYTHING in between


Tonight I'm your headliner

Fellas I want to keep your heads aligned

Ladies do you like head with legs vertically

lined?

Aligning head from the back reverse cowgirl

is fine

Me? I prefer getting headlined while headlining

at the same time.

… that's that 69

See… I want to get too personal with all of you.

Talking shit and speaking nasty

How taboo

I'm just up here doing some head aligning and

telling naughty truths

Don't be judgemental
Because I know that
Some of you
Are just as nasty!!!
You know how?
You are drinking the juice of my fruit
right now
take another sip of
*Assata right now
-that's a triple entendre

I am Queen Assata
I've talked like this for a looong time
The only thing new is this poem
It's being spoken for the first time
I wrote this for you tonight
I think I will name it
"Assata speaking out of line…
again"

Allow me to introduce myself
I write poetry
I write short stories
Tonight I have a drink named after me

Do me a favor and sip it slowly

I like my flavors hung

Come get sprung

off the verbal lashes

from my tongue.

I am Queen Assata

# *I am fucking a handsome Politician*

I am fucking a Politician

I can't tell you his name

but I can vouch

he is very passionate

on subjects regarding me and policy change

but when I try to discuss work

he tells me to stay in my lane

when I met him he had our

situation prearranged

He wanted nothing serious

just for me to fulfill his hunger games

Our politician is super sincere

on issues of laying that thang

and when he's inside of me

he never smiles he puts

terrorists to shame.

he fucked me in his office closet

and I didn't cum out the same

See he hits the political trail hard
and then stamps
his name
He has my vote
This territory he can claim
Yeah I'm fucking a political figure
if I told you who
it would put me to shame
Our relationship has been nothing
but pleasure and pain
I watch as he gives speeches from the mouth
that licked my ass on the plane
After meetings with world leaders
its me that eases his tension
He fingers me while on conference
calls discussing workers pensions
At this point his election is at
hopeful pace
I will keep his service secret
unless he tries to pull out of this race.

# I fucked up and fucked my barber

I fucked up and fucked my barber

That's when the problems started

in a way

he used to lay my hair

then I started

letting him lay into my vajayjay

I fucked around and fucked my barber

Cross contaminated the situation I

must say

I mixed the client barber privileges

Now I am trying to keep the situation

at bay

I fucked my Barber Tuesday then

forgot my appointment on Friday

He texted and asked if I was cumming

I said yeah I'm on my way

When I got there he sat me in the chair

but not to cut my hair only to foreplay

I fucked up and fucked my barber

I admit it was a bad decision but
the way he lined me up
I felt he had the right precision
when he cuts my hair he presses hard
against me through his true religions
but I can't get a good haircut anymore
because now he has cloudy vision

I fucked up and fucked my barber-yeah
I chose wrong.
Which head I needed him to
tend to
should have kept it
business all along.

#seekingnewbarber

# He called my bluff

He tried to call my bluff after
I read him Ear Candy
And had to remind him playfully
the characters in the story are fiction
not about me

Believe me, I wrote Ear Candy
stories fictionally
but he didn't believe it so I had to
say it repeatedly
He was so turned on
I gave him one round but it
turned to four
We went from the bed, to the counter,
on the couch to the floor
OMG I had to stop him he
had me feeling sore

He called my bluff

but I told him that I just write

but after he read Ear Candy

his eyes burned with excite


This man called my bluff

When I told him that he

wasn't fucking me enough

He also remember when I wrote

that *she* liked it tough

He got really rough

I had to tell myself shush

When he called my bluff

I had to tell him enough!!!


#thestoriesarenotaboutme

# Confessions of a Working Girl #13

As far as the sex last night

The tongue was better than the dick

Which made the experience alright

The licks were with passion

He showed up with an appetite

Then he put his gloves on and

his tongue and my pussy had a fight

I received a sample of the hammer

But he kept my buffet open all night

Things may have went left

considering that I fucked him

out of spite.

but honestly

the vengeful dick I received this afternoon

Had nothing on the pussy from last night

# Making Poetry

Making love to me is poetry

Sometime spoken softly

Often released loudly

Releasing into me

Lyrical bars into my sea

Diving into the wettest luxury

words and feelings of divinity

You will be poetry

that flows through me

# Realism

People wonder if my stories are real
The difference between Nonfiction and Fiction
is confessing the seal
Is this book full of my passionate reels?
Or a menu on how I devour
my meals
Are these stories reflecting
my closing of deals?
Or just fantasies for
time to kill
Though it's true I have made
characters kneel
I am a gentle wombman
so names I won't spill
The only way you'll know
if they are real
Is if you make
the story come to life
for you to feel.

— Realism

*You are Released*